Dogs

Cocker Spaniels

by Connie Colwell Miller

Consulting Editor: Gail Saunders-Smith, PhD

Consultant: Jennifer Zablotny, DVM
Member, American Veterinary Medical Association

Capstone press
Mankato, Minnesota

Pebble Books are published by Capstone Press,
151 Good Counsel Drive, P.O. Box 669, Mankato, Minnesota 56002.
www.capstonepress.com

1 2 3 4 5 6 12 11 10 09 08 07

Library of Congress Cataloging-in-Publication Data
Miller, Connie Colwell, 1976–
    Cocker spaniels / by Connie Colwell Miller.
    p. cm.—(Pebble Books. Dogs)
    Summary: "Simple text and photographs present the cocker spaniel breed and
how to care for them"—Provided by publisher.
    Includes bibliographical references and index.
    ISBN-13: 978-0-7368-6700-9 (hardcover)
    ISBN-10: 0-7368-6700-7 (hardcover)
    1. Cocker spaniels—Juvenile literature. I. Title. II. Series.
SF429.C55M49 2007
636.752'4—dc22   2006020520

Note to Parents and Teachers

The Dogs set supports national science standards related to life
science. This book describes and illustrates cocker spaniels. The
images support early readers in understanding the text. The
repetition of words and phrases helps early readers learn new
words. This book also introduces early readers to subject-specific
vocabulary words, which are defined in the Glossary section. Early
readers may need assistance to read some words and to use the
Table of Contents, Glossary, Read More, Internet Sites, and Index
sections of the book.

Table of Contents

Sweet Faces

Cocker spaniels are cheerful dogs.
Their sweet faces make them popular pets.

Cocker spaniels have
soft, silky coats.
Long, floppy ears hang
from their heads.
They wag their
stumpy tails.

From Puppy to Adult

Cocker spaniel puppies
are born with long tails.
Most owners dock
the tails when the puppies
are a few days old.

Young cocker spaniels enjoy learning new things. They learn to play fetch. They learn to sniff out and follow trails.

Adult cocker spaniels are lively. They play with their families.

14

Cocker Spaniel Care

Cocker spaniels have long coats that tangle easily. Owners should brush their dogs every day. Cocker spaniels need haircuts every six weeks.

Cocker spaniels' long ears get dirty easily. Owners should clean their dogs' ears every day.

Cocker spaniels
can become pudgy
without exercise.
Owners should walk
their dogs each day.

Cocker spaniels
make great pets.
They bring joy to their
owners for many years.

Glossary

coat—a dog's fur

dock—to cut a dog's tail short

fetch—to go after something and bring it back

lively—full of life and energy

pudgy—plump or chubby

stumpy—short and thick

tangle—to twist together in a confused mass

trail—a smell left behind by a person or animal

Read More

Bozzo, Linda. *My First Dog.* My First Pet Library.
Berkeley Heights, N.J.: Enslow, 2007.

Murray, Julie. *Cocker Spaniels.* Animal Kingdom.
Edina, Minn.: ABDO, 2005.

Internet Sites

FactHound offers a safe, fun way to find Internet sites
related to this book. All of the sites on FactHound have
been researched by our staff.

Here's how:

1. Visit *www.facthound.com*
2. Choose your grade level.
3. Type in this book ID **0736867007** for
   age-appropriate sites. You may also browse subjects by
   clicking on letters, or by clicking on pictures and words.
4. Click on the **Fetch It** button.

FactHound will fetch the best sites for you!

Index

Word Count: 146
Grade: 1
Early-Intervention Level: 16

Editorial Credits
Martha E. H. Rustad, editor; Juliette Peters, set designer; Kyle Grenz, book designer; Kara Birr, photo researcher; Scott Thoms, photo editor

Photo Credits
Brenda Fry, San Angelo, TX, 12; Capstone Press/Karon Dubke, 14, 16; Cheryl A. Ertelt, 6; Getty Images Inc./Asia Images/Alex Mares-Manton, 18; Kent Dannen, 8; Mark Raycroft, cover, 1; PhotoEdit Inc./Myrleen Ferguson Cate, 20; Shutterstock/Aleksander Bochenek, 10; Shutterstock/Claudia Steininger, 4

TE DUE